Go Fish!

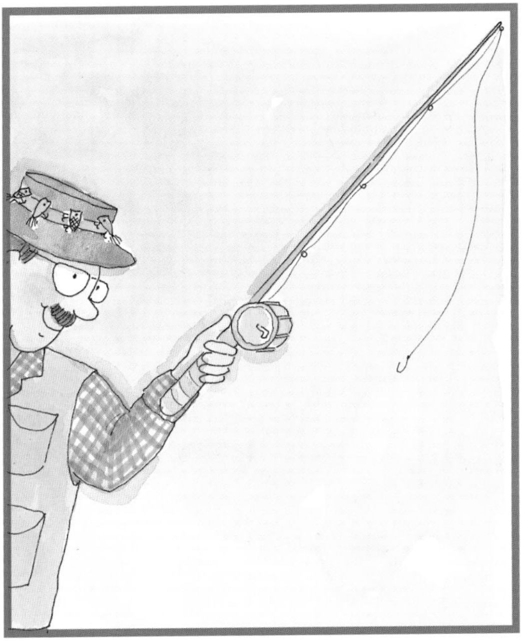

Written by L.R. Kelly
Illustrated by Shelley Dieterichs

Scott Foresman

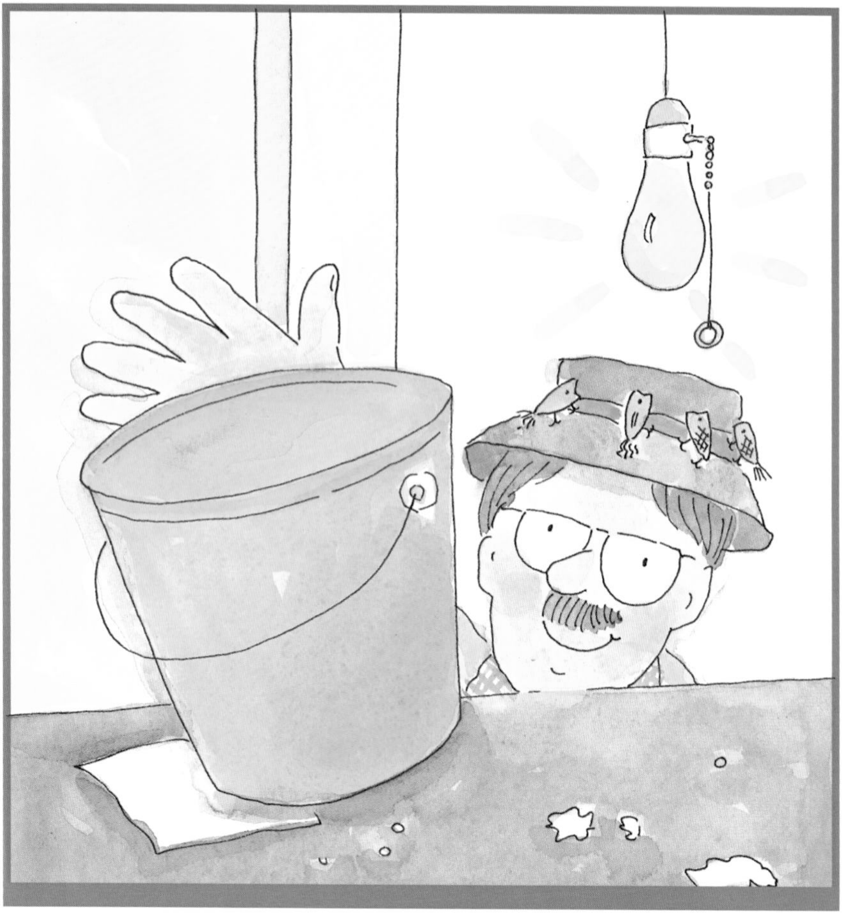

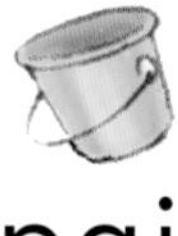

pail

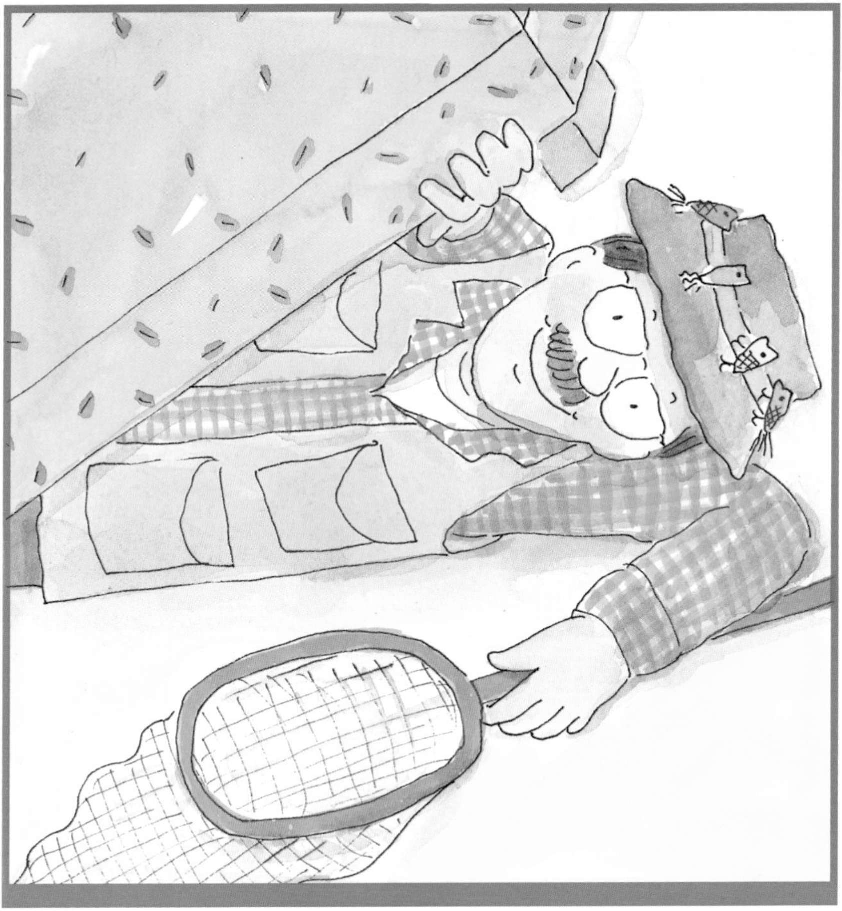

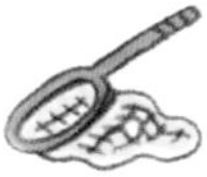

net

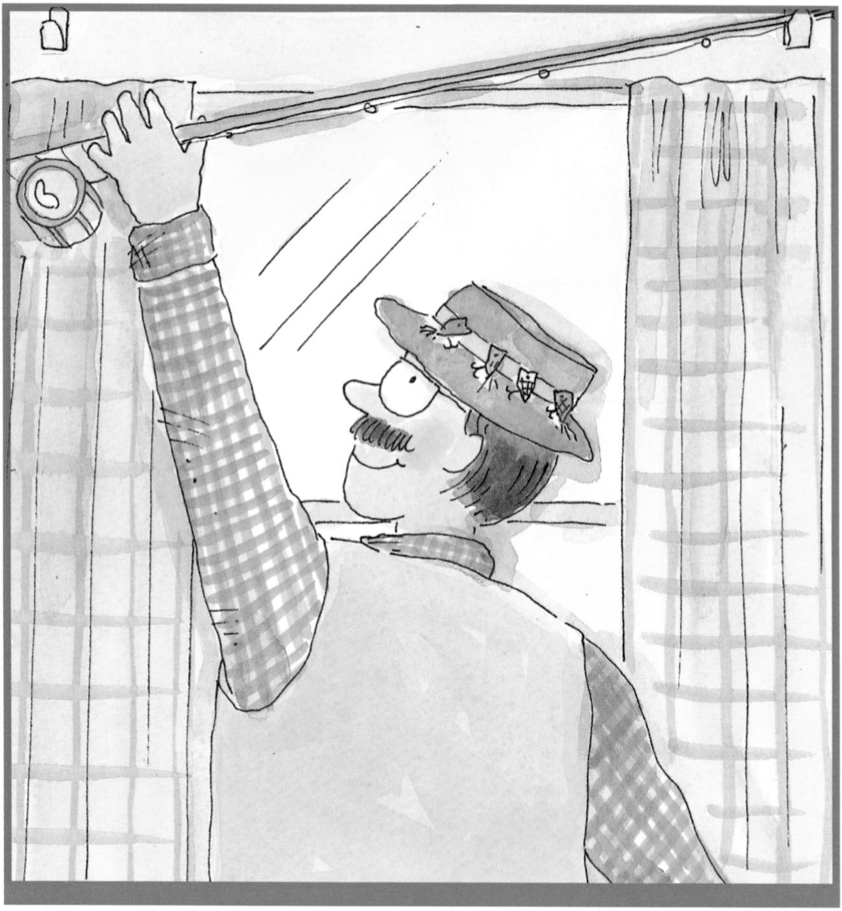

pole

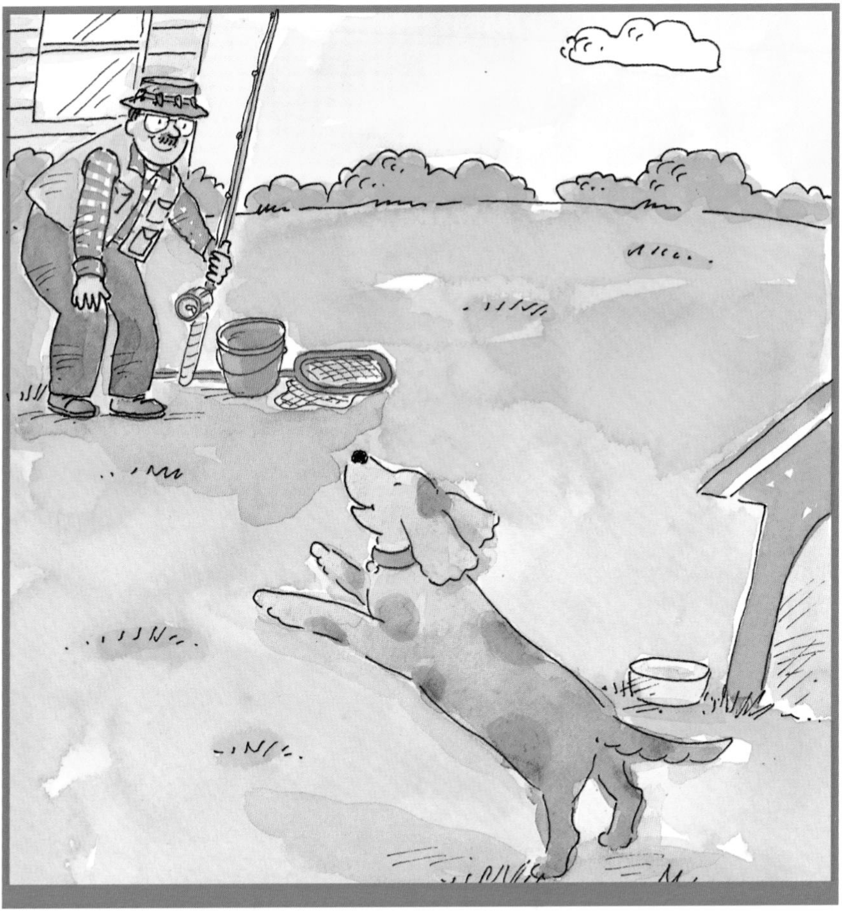

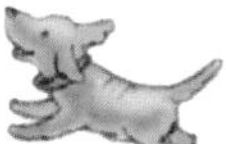

dog

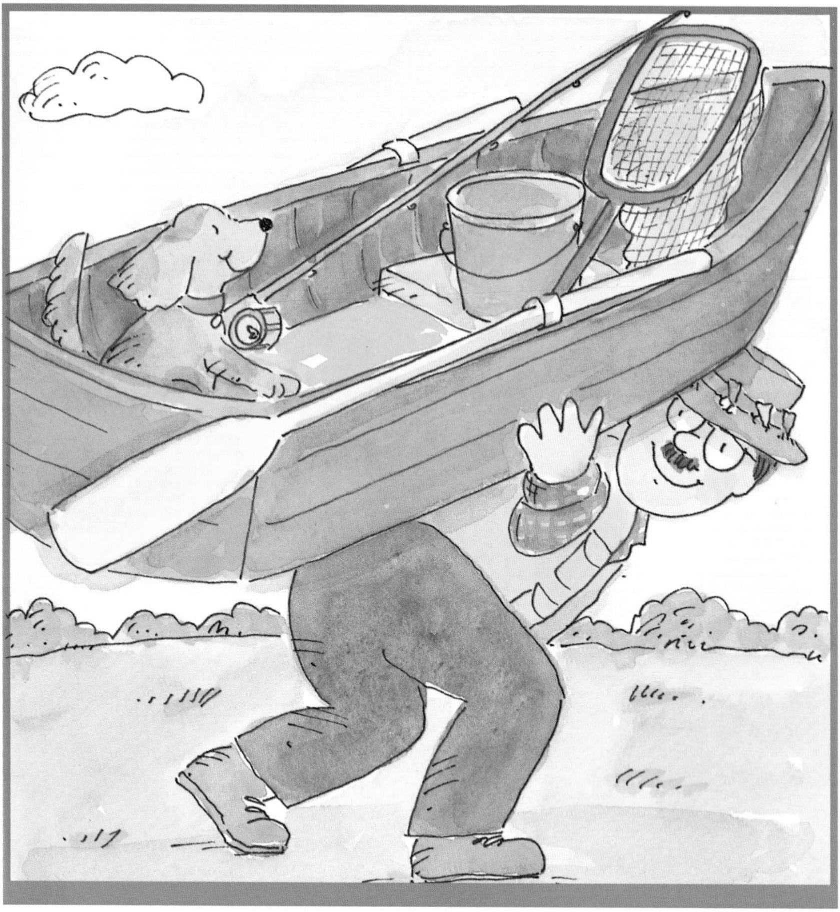

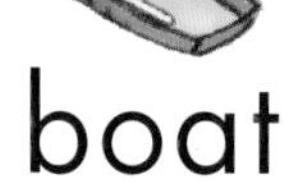

boat

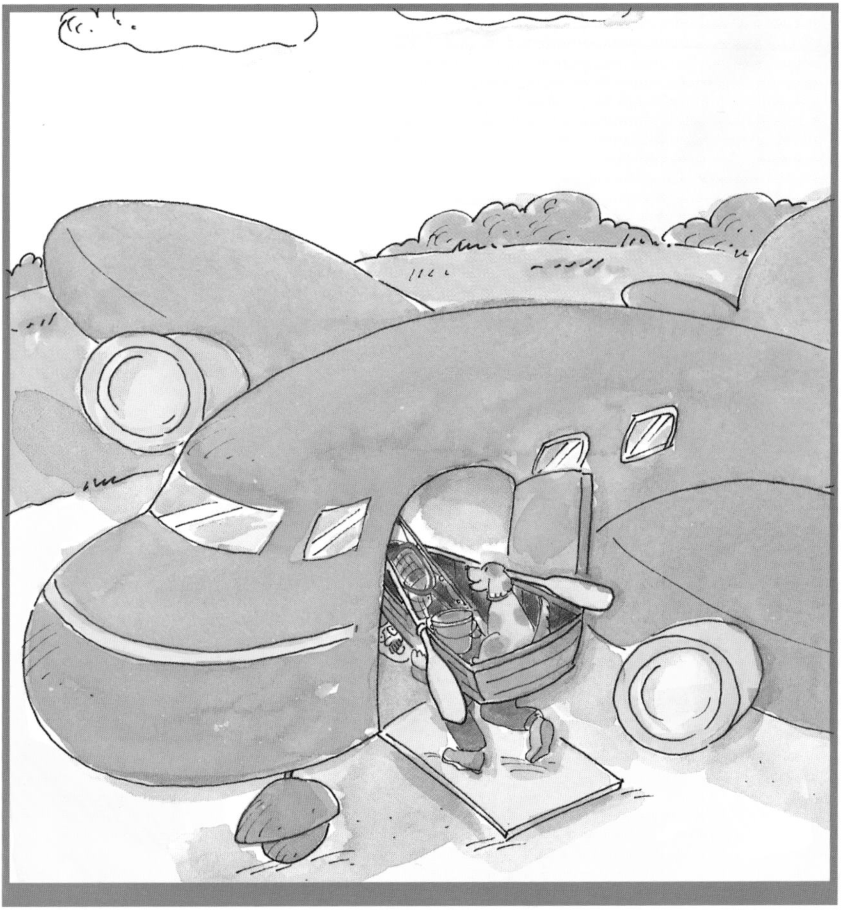

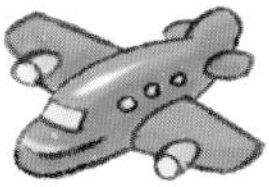

plane

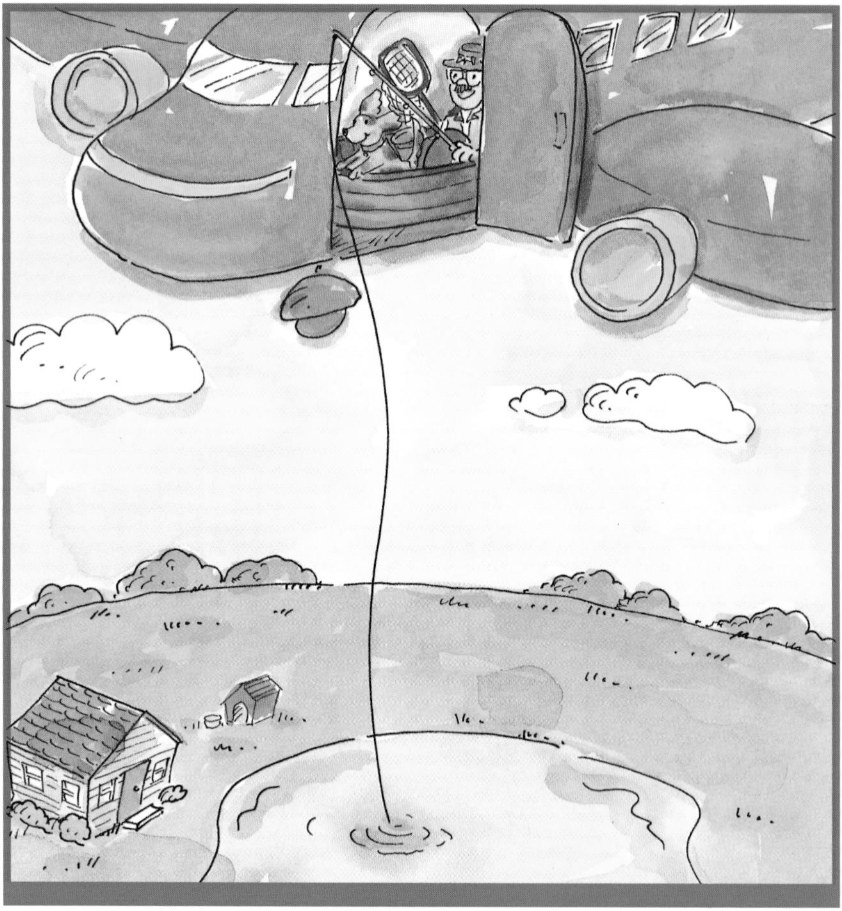

Go fish!